# Memories

Also by Lang Leav

*Love & Misadventure*
*Lullabies*

# Memories

### LANG LEAV

Andrews McMeel
Publishing®

a division of Andrews McMeel Universal

Andrews McMeel Publishing
a division of Andrews McMeel Universal
1130 Walnut Street, Kansas City, Missouri 64106

www.andrewsmcmeel.com

16 17 18 19 20 SDB 10 9 8 7 6 5 4 3

ISBN: 978-1-4494-7239-9

Library of Congress Control Number: 2015939470

*The Fell Types are digitally reproduced by Igino Marini.
www.iginomarini.com*

ATTENTION: SCHOOLS AND BUSINESSES
Andrews McMeel books are available at quantity discounts
with bulk purchase for educational, business, or sales
promotional use. For information, please e-mail the
Andrews McMeel Publishing Special Sales Department:
specialsales@amuniversal.com.

*For Michael*

*Reading you has made me
a better writer.*

*Loving you has made me
a better person.*

*Forget her tattered memories, or the pages others took;
you are her ever after—the hero of her book.*

# CONTENTS

# Introduction

*I am hopelessly in love with a memory. An echo from another time, another place.*
—Michael Faudet

*Memories* is a collection of poetry and prose, hand selected from my two previous books, *Love & Misadventure* and *Lullabies*. It also features some new writing I have completed over the last year.

My intention was to create a book that is enduring, one that could be kept as a keepsake or given to someone special in your life.

I have always thought of memories as fragments, like colored glass shards in a kaleidoscope. It is the source of great beauty in our lives, yet the cause of such heartache. It remains the bridge between our past and present—it gives weight and dimension to our very existence.

I hope you enjoy *Memories* as much as I enjoyed putting it together. I know there are many great moments that are yet to transpire for you. I hope in time, you will find echoes of them in this book.

Much love,
Lang

PART ONE

*Here and Now*

## The Rose

Have you ever loved a rose,
    and watched her slowly bloom;
    and as her petals would unfold,
    you grew drunk on her perfume.

Have you ever seen her dance,
    her leaves all wet with dew;
    and quivered with a new romance—
    the wind, he loved her too.

Have you ever longed for her,
    on nights that go on and on;
    for now, her face is all a blur,
    like a memory kept too long.

Have you ever loved a rose,
    and bled against her thorns;
    and swear each night to let her go,
    then love her more by dawn.

## STOWAWAY

I love the way he looks at me. Shy and half-cocked as though he is caught off guard, like he is retracing his steps to remember all the ways to make me smile. He brings me flowers every Sunday and tells me stories about mermaids and sirens with their sharp claws and beguiling lips. He says I remind him of the sea and attaches me to a metaphor I've never heard before, when I thought I must have heard them all. I think someone broke his heart once and now he can't bear to be apart from the ocean. He said it's strange how the smallest things can wreck a ship. Like a rock, or a wave, or a hairline crack in the hull. He calls me his little stowaway and he says it sadly, tenderly, as though I can sink him.

## Birthdays

It is a ceremony, the blowing of candles, the cutting of a cake—the mess of cream and sponge in your mouth. The taste is sweet and familiar, like a newly formed wish, fashioned from all the ones you've made before.

You don't remember them in sequence—the things you ask for. You only recall those you wanted the most. Like the pair of neon pink roller skates you saw in the shop window when you were twelve. How deeply you felt their absence when you sat among the litter of torn wrapping paper and empty new possessions.

Or the year you turned sixteen; when your best friend's mother got really sick, and all you wanted was for her to be okay again. It was the year you learned that shooting stars were either a blessing or a curse, depending on what you wanted to believe.

Then there was that year you fell in love. The one where there weren't any candles—just you walking late at night through the city streets with your heart in pieces, wanting to give yourself to the first stranger who called you beautiful.

Since then it's been the same every year. As soon as the first match is struck, the smell of burning takes you backward through your memory. It stops you right at that moment on that warm, September night, as you watched the first trickle of melting wax hit the icing, and you couldn't think of a single damn thing you wanted—because he was standing there, in the flickering light, asking you to make a wish.

## Poetry

I know you have seen things you wish you hadn't. You have done things you wish you could take back. And you wonder why you were thrown into the thick of it all—why you had to suffer the way you did. And as you are sitting there alone and hurting, I wish I could put a pen in your hand and gently remind you how the world has given you poetry and now you must give it back.

## Numbers

Nothing felt like mine anymore, not after you. All those little things that defined me; small sentimental trinkets, car keys, pin codes, and passwords. They all felt like you. And more than anything else, my number—the one you boldly asked for that night, amidst a sea of people, under a sky of talking satellites and glowing stars.

You said no matter how many times you erased me from your phone, you would still recognize that number when it flashed on your screen. The series of sixes and nines, like the dip of my waist to the curve of my hips, your hands pressed into the small of my back. Nines and sixes that were reminiscent of two contented cats, curled together like a pair of speech marks. You said if you could never hold me or kiss me again, you could live with that. But you couldn't bear the thought of us not speaking and asked, at the very least, could I just allow you that one thing?

I wonder what went through your mind the day you dialed my number to find it had been disconnected. If your imagination had raced with thoughts of what new city I had run to and who was sharing my bed. Isn't it strange how much of our lives are interchangeable, how little is truly ours. Someone else's ring tone, someone else's song, someone else's words, someone else's broken heart. These are the things we inherit by choice or by chance.

And it wasn't my choice to love you but it was mine to leave. I don't think the moon ever meant to be a satellite, kept in loving orbit, locked in hopeless inertia, destined to repeat the same pattern over and over—to meet in eclipse with the sun—only when the numbers allowed.

## A Writer's Muse

One day he will find you. He will touch you and you will feel a lifetime of indifference—of apathy melt away in a single moment. And you will ache for him. You will love him, in the way you walk a tightrope—in the way people learn to fall asleep in a war zone. You will bleed for him until the day he is gone. You will bleed for him every day after that. The time will pass and you will feel robbed—and you will grow bitter. You will ask why, but you won't get an answer. And that is when the words will come.

## THE STRANGER

Does it make you crazy? To think he saw you—his eyes passed over you and if only there had been some small mishap in that pivotal moment. A spilled drink, a stumble through the door—his hand reaching out to steady you and it would have happened. A whole new world would have opened up like a vortex to swallow you both into blissful delirium. But you turned away, out of shyness or indecision and by the time you turned back, he was gone.

How do you explain it without sounding unsound? That click you felt when your eyes met his, like the switch of a train track, transporting you for one miraculous moment, to what might have been.

Then reality intervenes and with a shake of your head, you tell yourself to stop chasing shadows. But I can tell you now—what you felt was real—and you must always listen to that click. For it is the sound of your fate beckoning. It is the voice of your destiny calling. Sometimes it only calls once.

## After the Storm

There are storms that change the skyline, that leave patches of blue where branches had once spread their brittle fingers. And in the aftermath, an eerie calm settles over the forest, as shell-shocked birds sing warily in the sunlight. The nervous flutter of their injured wings, barely audible above the hammering of a hummingbird's heart.

You once told me the wind is silent. How his sound can only be heard through collision. Last night, he cried with a violent yearning while he tore through the trees. As he brought down their twisted branches, I thought of the first time you said my name.

You were the storm that changed the skyline. After the damage and the deluge, I could see things so much clearer. There hasn't been another like you since.

In 1953, we began naming hurricanes so we could remember them beyond the wreckage. So we could try to make sense of the destruction. This is the way I remember you.

## Memories

Have you ever felt it? That split second before the feeling catches the memory—that small haven of neutrality, before the headlong crash into recognition. Your mind pulls him to the foreground like a snapped rubber band. And you think of the line he drew in the sand, the one you can't seem to put a foot past. Like a tripwire, you're afraid of the damage but you know you can't keep standing still. And the world falls away and you're exactly where you were on the last night you saw him, when he had his hands in your hair and his mouth on your neck and he never said a word about leaving.

## Now and Then

I was always meant for you. With my tennis shoes and wild hair, dragging a case with a cello hidden between its velvet walls. Even then.

I was always meant for you. In my black woolen dress and sapphire studs. Between hotel rooms and standing ovations. Even now.

I was never meant for road signs with foreign names, or lovers who spoke in exotic tongues. For maps that were composed in a language I could not read and printed in a dialect I could not write.

You said I was like a bird of prey, caged by my captors and made to sing love songs to the sky. You said my sadness was like the sun, beautiful from a distance but it hurt you too much to come closer.

I was never meant for poetry. For words carved into history, like ancient runes that told the same tragic tale over and over. If any historian were to decipher the symbols hammered into stone, they would say I was meant for you. Even before the first mallet had struck iron, even after all civilization has crumbled into dust and the sky is set alight with a thousand exploding stars—even then.

## A Love Story

Beyond the shores of melancholy,
    there was a time I held your hand.
    My heart now bears an untold story,
    like a ship at sea, that longs for land.

A great untruth, my lips have borrowed,
    a boundless treasure to line my chest;
    the wealth of words are in their sorrow—
    and words are all I can bequest.

We will remain unwritten through history,
    no X will mark us on the map;
    but in books of prose and poetry,
    you loved me once, in a paragraph.

And your love has left me, on this island,
    it has filled my cup up to the brink;
    yet I grow thirsty in this silence—
    there is not a drop for me to drink.

## Virtual Love

We fell in love through screens, through satellites that carried our words across the aching void. Night after night, we spoke about hands on bodies and lips on skin. After the silence, I would think of all the girls made of flesh and bone within your arm's reach.

As winter gave way to summer, the dust motes dancing in the sunlight blurred into pixels, and I gave my heart to a photograph. I wondered how I could be so afraid of losing something that wasn't mine.

Then came the crossed wires, the signal jam. The static that grew between us—its dull, murmuring protest. And I would question if there were others just like me, who had found themselves caught in your orbit. Whether I was just another celestial body, sent up from the ground; when the moon—the original satellite—is the only one you see from where you're standing.

## A Writer's Plea

Take me someplace where I can feel something—I want to give away my heart. Tell me his name so I can know love when it speaks to me. Give me someone I can write about.

## In the End

I was ready to give it all up—everything. I was half out of my mind with love. And I didn't think twice about what I was throwing into the fire, as long as I could keep it burning for just another minute—if only I was allowed to sit awhile longer beside its pale glow.

That was how I loved you in the end. With my body cold and shuddering. With empty hands over smoldering ash, counting out the minutes.

## Pieces of You

He knows I can't tell a joke without laughing. And how I'm always talking about second chances. He knows I sleep all day and wake up tired. And I could never give anyone a straight answer.

I cried the first time I told him about you. I said I was sorry as he held me so close. He said he now knew why my eyes were like searchlights. How they looked at the sky with such longing. And why I read my stars in the paper each morning.

He left me one Sunday with his cup half empty. I padded downstairs and saw the writing on the wall. Outside the rain was already falling. And there were still pieces of you behind every door.

## SHE

She was the sound of glass shattering—the sharp ringing in your ears. The perpetual motion of a spinning ballerina trapped inside a music box. The sad, tinny tune of La Vie en Rose.

She was the zigzag in your straight line. The absence in your direction. She was every turn you took when racing through a hedge maze, against the setting sun.

She was the tide that came in and out, like the breath of the wounded. She was the blood that flowed between heart and head.

She was the book that was not written. The sentence that was not scripted. She was the word you wished you could have said.

## Reaching Out

I have given so much to things that weren't worth my time. When all along, it's the people I love that I should have carried. It's the ones I cared for whom I should have been responsible.

But maybe I'm too late. Because I don't know how to talk to you. I don't know how to ask you if you're okay. I don't know how to tell you I am so afraid of losing you. How much light would leave my life if you were no longer part of it.

I just hope you realize how much you mean to me. I just wish I could remind you of how beautiful you are. I'm sorry I haven't told you in so long. But please don't think I have given up on you. I will never give up on you. My arms are wide open. There is always a place for you here.

## Faith

I whisper your name like a prayer—with all the hope of heaven.

I trace the lines of your palm and draw a map to salvation.

I hear the knock of your heart and I answer it like my calling.

## HOME

Do you think of me on airplanes? With your headphones snug around your ears and the clouds below? Do you think of my hands as you are exploring new territory—the freedom, the thrill, the rush? When you travel against the turn of our planet, does it take you back into the past?

I think of you on jet planes. In thoughts that go a million miles an hour. Over toy towns and towers made of tin. Nothing feels real without you.

Do you think of what could have been? In the early morning light when you wake up next to some stranger, wondering why you don't feel a thing. In every bar room and bedroom where you're forced into conversation or giving away parts of yourself—do you miss me?

Do you think of me in cars? When every turn you take is driving us further apart. Does every road sign pleading you to take care, remind you of how much I want you, how deeply you are loved?

I think of you on roads that stretch into the horizon. On roundabouts and signs that keep telling me I am going in the wrong direction. I hope you think of me as much as I think of you. I hope that every step will bring you closer, that every dead end is a messenger, willing you to turn back around, reminding you it's time to come home.

## Waiting

I try to think of a word that is closest to love and the only thing that comes to mind is your name. I try to imagine what I would say if our paths ever crossed again but I keep drawing a blank.

I've forgotten what it was like to feel the sun on my skin without worrying that it could hurt me. I've stopped throwing myself from cliffs, with my arms in the air, waiting for the splash below.

Every day, I look in the mirror and I see more and more of my mother's face staring back at me. Every day I measure the weight of my past against the present and feel the drag of what could have been.

I find a photograph of you and wonder when I'll stop hoping. I stare at the clock, with its slow methodical hands and dread the day when I'll know it's too late.

## Dear Love

Love, he has abandoned me,
    do with me as you will.
    Love, he left—unceremoniously,
    why must I love him still?

The best of me I gave to him—
    the years, the days, the hours.
    Precious little, in turn he'd given,
    like dew to a wilting flower.

Love, he sheared away tenderly,
    my beauty, my strength, my mind,
    the gifts that were bestowed to me—
    were swallowed in his pride.

Love, has he forgotten me?
    Please tell me what you've heard,
    I guard his memory jealously—
    with him I'd placed my worth.

## Revelation

Here is the place where you found me. Under the half-moon and its half-light. You said, if only I had met you there that night. Perhaps we could have found our way. I learned something about sadness after that day.

You showed me insanity, as you promised you would. Like an open window, seven storeys high. And it was just as terrible and as beautiful as you and I.

And you said ecstasy was a storm cloud, just before the rain would burst into the night sky, like a thousand aquatic stars— and not one single moment before. And you were right. You were right about it all.

## Language

I remember learning the alphabet. How those strange markings, alien and incoherent, grew more and more familiar, like the name of someone you love.

The moment words found me, they burrowed themselves into my bones, they settled like dust in my lungs until I felt them every time I breathed in and out. I would place them side by side like fractals, in a myriad of verse.

I remember learning your name, the strange jumble of letters that danced under my tongue, that leapt from my hungry mouth. Those four syllables that bit deep into my soul like poetry. I remember how I whispered them against your lips.

And you would say, *this is how I am with you, with you.*

It was words that I fell for. In the end, it was words that broke my heart.

## A Poem

I wrote a poem about a girl who loves you. I said a soliloquy that was spoken in her honor.

I felt every word that burst from her lips, like shooting stars, into the air around us. If it were possible to hold love in your hand, it was her hand that trembled as I held it.

I could taste her tears that ran like rain on windshields. The kind that searched with longing, for lonely drop after drop, to form a pool of forlorn belonging.

I wrote this poem for the girl who loves you—for she loves you more than I love you. Because she is sorry and so am I.

## In Love

You've not yet had your heart in halves,
　　so little do you know of love—
　　to tell me I will soon forget,
　　there will be others to regret.

Now all the years have proved you wrong,
　　my love for him burns bright and strong;
　　you can't divide the stars from night—
　　from love there can be no respite.

## Sunday Best

Do you remember that night I turned up on your doorstep?
I was wearing my Sunday best. You watched the mascara as it
ran down like fault lines, and you knew I had blood on my lips.

*I'm tired of running,* I said—

and the earth shook a little.

*So am I,* you replied

as it shook a little more.

*I don't want anyone else,* I whispered.

And I felt myself crumble.

You held out your arms and I was cracked porcelain. We
looked at each other as we stood at the precipice. And I knew
once I fell, I'd never stop falling. And everything before
you would be time to kill. You said you were scared but you
couldn't ignore it.

And that was the moment when we became real.

## Hope

One day you walk into a cafe and there he is. It's as simple as that. As easy as that. Then forever after, you spend your life, walking into cafes, hoping he'll magically appear. Like he did the first time. Or there would be someone else, just like him, sitting, with his head buried in a book. He would turn to look at you and it would all begin again.

When love finds you, it doesn't come with crashing waves or thunderbolts. It appears as a song on the radio or a particular blue in the sky. It dawns on you slowly, like a warm winter sunrise—where the promise of summer shines out from within.

We number our days and divide our seasons. We endlessly define what it is to be in love. When in truth, spring blurs into summer and always has, long before that line was ever drawn. Your love for him is the same—it runs wild and free. Like the air around you, it stretches all across the world, it does not leave a single thing untouched. You carry that love with you, like a bright and blazing beacon, a straight line from your heart to his. And it keeps alive that aching, throbbing hope, that somewhere in the world, there is a cafe and within those walls, he is there, hoping just as much as you.

## Stardust

If you came to me with a face I have not seen, with a voice I have never heard, I would still know you. Even if centuries separated us, I would still feel you. Somewhere between the sand and the stardust, through every collapse and creation, there is a pulse that echoes of you and I.

When we leave this world, we give up all our possessions and our memories. Love is the only thing we take with us. It is all we carry from one life to the next.

## New Light

When goodbye was said,
    there it began
    the careful tread—
    the ones you chose
    to love instead.

Yet inside you glows
    a candle lit
    those years ago
    and brighter still
    it burns for him
    a searing flame
    to stave the dark
    you hold within.

The honor the promise
    you once made—
    when you and he
    were skin to skin,
    and the brightest star
    had ceased its reign—
    to herald new light,
    born in his name.

## HAPPINESS

I know my being happy is an anomaly. No one knows me better than you. But I can say without avoiding your gaze, without crossing my fingers behind my back; or the other things I do when speaking untruthfully—I am happy. I know the rain does not discriminate between day or night and either will hold its own light and dark—but now, at this very moment, I feel like I am the sun. And I know in my heart, I will always look upon this time—not without a sense of melancholy— that it was the happiest in my life.

## The Saddest Thing

There was someone I knew, a long time ago. I was so in love with him I couldn't see straight. The saddest thing is, he felt the same way about me.

It was easy in the beginning. All we had to do was laugh at the same things and love took over and did the rest. I had never felt so connected to another person.

He would always say it felt as though I was made for him. How glad he was to have met me. We were so sure of what we felt. We should have held tight, onto that certainty.

There is never one particular reason why two people are torn apart. All these years later, I have stopped looking for answers. I know better now, that love is never a guarantee. Not when you have the rest of the world to contend with.

Sometimes you have to step back and look at these things from a philosophical standpoint. And I know loving him has taught me something about myself, it has broadened my understanding of the world. And if it has done the same for him, then it wasn't all in vain.

## THE NIGHT

It's been a while since words have found me,
 the time between—you'll come and go;
 I'd grown to love the sun around me,
 I've been a stranger to my woe.

It's been so long since there was silence,
 all around me, your voice had rung;
 like a bird who sings to greet the morning,
 to tell you that the day has come.

It's been some time since I've felt lonely,
 like a book that is no longer read;
 the darkness lingers on without you,
 it fills my empty heart with dread.

It seems an age ago, since you have left me,
 time has filled me, with words unsaid;
 as the sadness seeps into me slowly,
 and I am left to face the night ahead.

## Her

There is so much history in the way he looks at her. In the way he says her name. When they are together, there is a current that runs between them; like an electric charge on the verge of erupting into a perfect storm.

*I don't love her anymore*, he says.

And it is in the way he says the word *her*—that tells me otherwise.

## Love

I don't know what it is like to love someone who the world tells me I am not supposed to love. I can't imagine how hard it must be to love someone I am afraid to kiss on the street.

But I do know what it is like to love someone who I cannot be with. I know how it feels to have my brain tell me one thing, and my heart another. I know how hard it is to have to love someone in secret. To live with the knowledge that if circumstances had been different, I would be with the one I love.

I do know there are all kinds of barriers to love. I do believe the world needs less of them.

## Collision

Do you think I have slipped into a time warp?

It was your opening line. I didn't know it then, but my past, present, and future were set to collide.

At the time, the collision felt like a gentle wake-up call. Like a lazy Sunday morning spent gently parting ways with sleep. But now when I look back, I see it for what it was—alarm bells blaring at five a.m. and a plane I couldn't miss.

I got lost in the day to day. I passed by prophets on the city streets with their signs, warning me about the apocalypse. I never imagined it was walking right beside me, holding my hand. Night after night, I looked into your eyes but never once did they offer me a prelude to the destruction.

Life went on without you. Of course, it did. Of course, it does. It was just an ending, they tell me, not the end.

PART TWO

*Remember When*

## A Toast!

To new beginnings,
    in fear and faith
    and all it tinges.

To love is a dare,
    when hope and despair,
    are gates upon it hinges.

## Three Questions

*What was it like to love him?* asked Gratitude.
It was like being exhumed, I answered. And brought to life in
a flash of brilliance.

*What was it like to be loved in return?* asked Joy.
It was like being seen after a perpetual darkness, I replied. To
be heard after a lifetime of silence.

*What was it like to lose him?* asked Sorrow.
There was a long pause before I responded:

It was like hearing every good-bye ever said to me—said all
at once.

## My Heart

Perhaps I never loved enough,
    If only I'd loved much more;
    I would not nearly had so much,
    left waiting, for you in store.

If I had given away my heart—
    to those who came before;
    it would be safer left in parts—
    but now you have it all.

## Love Lost

There is one who you belong to,
    whose love—there is no song for.
    And though you know it's wrongful,
    there is someone else you long for.

Your heart was once a vessel,
    it was filled up to the brim;
    until the day he left you,
    now everything sings of him.

Of the two who came to love you,
    to one, your heart you gave.
    He lives in stars above you—
    in the love who came and stayed.

## After You

If I wrote it in a book,
    could I shelve it?

If I told of what you took,
    would that help it?

If I will it,
    can I un-feel it,
    now I've felt it?

## Rogue Planets

As a kid, I would count backwards from ten and imagine at one, there would be an explosion—perhaps caused by a rogue planet crashing into Earth or some other major catastrophe. When nothing happened, I'd feel relieved and at the same time, a little disappointed.

I think of you at ten; the first time I saw you. Your smile at nine and how it lit up something inside me I had thought long dead. Your lips at eight pressed against mine and at seven, your warm breath in my ear and your hands everywhere. You tell me you love me at six and at five we have our first real fight. At four we have our second and three, our third. At two you tell me you can't go on any longer and then at one, you ask me to stay.

And I am relieved, so relieved—and a little disappointed.

## PRETEXT

Our love——a dead star
    to the world it burns brightly——

    But it died long ago.

## Souls

When two souls fall in love, there is nothing else but the yearning to be close to the other. The presence that is felt through a hand held, a voice heard, or a smile seen.

Souls do not have calendars or clocks, nor do they understand the notion of time or distance. They only know it feels right to be with one another.

This is the reason why you miss someone so much when they are not there—even if they are only in the very next room. Your soul only feels their absence—it doesn't realize the separation is temporary.

. . . . . . . . . . . . . . . . . . . . . . . . . . . . . . . .

Can I ask you something?
Anything.
Why is it every time we say good night, it feels like good-bye?

## Some Time Out

The time may not
    be prime for us,
    though you are
    a special person.

We may be just
    two different clocks,
    that do not tock,
    in unison.

## The Wanderer

What is she like?
I was told—
she is a
melancholy soul.

She is like
the sun to night;
a momentary gold.

A star when dimmed
by dawning light;
the flicker of
a candle blown.

A lonely kite
lost in flight—
someone once
had flown.

## Sad Things

*Why do you write sad things?* he asked. *When I am here, when I love you.*

Because someday, in one way or another, you will be taken from me or I you. It is inevitable. But please understand; from the moment I met you, I stopped writing for the past. I no longer write for the present. When I write sad things, I am writing for the future.

## Sea of Strangers

In a sea of strangers,
　　you've longed to know me.
　　Your life spent sailing
　　to my shores.

The arms that yearn
　　to someday hold me,
　　will ache beneath
　　the heavy oars.

Please take your time
　　and take it slowly;
　　as all you do
　　will run its course.

And nothing else
　　can take what only—
　　was always meant
　　as solely yours.

## Broken Hearts

I know you've lost someone and it hurts. You may have lost them suddenly, unexpectedly. Or perhaps you began losing pieces of them until one day, there was nothing left. You may have known them all your life or you may have barely known them at all. Either way, it is irrelevant—you cannot control the depth of a wound another inflicts upon you.

Which is why I am not here to tell you tomorrow will be a new day. That the sun will go on shining. Or there are plenty of fish in the sea. What I will tell you is this; it's okay to be hurting as much as you are. What you are feeling is not only completely valid but necessary—because it makes you so much more human. And though I can't promise it will get better any time soon, I can tell you that it will—eventually. For now, all you can do is take your time. Take all the time you need.

## An Artist in Love

I drew him in my world;
 I write him in my lines,
 I want to be his girl,
 he was never meant as mine.

I drew him in my world;
 he is always on my mind;
 I draw his every line.
 It hurts when he's unkind.

I drew him in my world;
 I draw him all the time,
 but I don't know where
 to draw the line.

## The Seventh Sea

The answer is yes, always yes. I cannot deny you anything you ask. I will not let you bear the agony of not knowing.

Yes I love you, I swear it. On every grain of salt in the ocean— on all my tears. I found you when I reached the seventh sea, just as I had stopped looking.

It seems a lifetime ago that I began searching for you.

A lifetime of pain and sorrow. Of disappointment and missed opportunities.

All I had hoped for. All the things I can never get back.

When I am with you, I want for nothing.

## In Two Parts

You come and go so easily,
    your life is as you knew—
    while mine is split in two.

How I envy so the half of me,
    who lived before love's due,
    who was yet to know of you.

## A Question

It was a question I had worn on my lips for days—like a loose thread on my favorite sweater I couldn't resist pulling—despite knowing it could all unravel around me.

"Do you love me?" I ask.

In your hesitation I found my answer.

## A Dedication

She lends her pen,
    to thoughts of him,
    that flow from it,
    in her solitary.

For she is his poet,
    And he is her poetry.

## A Dream

As the Earth began spinning faster and faster, we floated upwards, hands locked tightly together, eyes sad and bewildered. We watched as our faces grew younger and realized the Earth was spinning in reverse, moving us backwards in time.

Then we reached a point where I no longer knew who you were and I was grasping the hands of a stranger. But I didn't let go. And neither did you.

. . . . . . . . . . . . . . . . . . . . . . . . . . . . . . . . .

I had my first dream about you last night.
Really? She smiles. What was it about?
I don't remember exactly, but the whole time I was dreaming, I knew you were mine.

## Fading Polaroid

My eyes were the first to forget. The face I once cradled between my hands, now a blur. And your voice is slowly drifting from my memory, like a fading polaroid. But the way I felt is still crystal clear. Like it was yesterday.

There are Philosophers who claim the past, present, and future all exist at the one time. And the way I have felt, the way I feel— that bittersweet ache between wanting and having—is evidence of their theory.

I felt you before I knew you and I still feel you now. And in that brief moment between—wrapped in your arms thinking, *how lucky I am, how lucky I am, how lucky I am—*

How lucky I was.

## Ode to Sorrow

Her eyes, a closed book,
　　her heart, a locked door;
　　she writes melancholy
　　like she's lived it before.

She once loved in a way,
　　you could not understand;
　　he left her in pieces
　　and a pen in her hand.

The ode to her sorrow
　　in the life she has led—
　　her scratches on paper,
　　the words they have bled.

## The Professor

A streak of light flashes across the sky. Thick heavy raindrops pound the uneven dirt floor, littered with dried leaves and twigs. She follows closely behind him, clutching an odd contraption—a rectangular device attached with a long, squiggly, antenna. "You were right about the storm, Professor!" she yells over the howling wind. "Yes, my assistant!" he cries, voice charged with excitement, as he holds up the long, metal conductor. She stumbles over a log as he reaches out to catch her.

They tumble on the dry grass laughing. He tosses aside the bent, silver coat hanger, wrapping his arms around her waist. The little transistor radio falls from her hands.

The sun peeks through the treetops.

She thinks of their first conversation. "I live by a forest," he said, describing it in such a way that when she came to scale those crooked, winding stairs, it was like she had seen it a thousand times before. As if it had always been there, waiting to welcome her. Like the pretty, sunlit room that remained unfurnished, sitting empty in his house, now filled with her paints and brushes.

She would fondly call him her Frankenstein, this man who was a patchwork of all the things she had ever longed for. He gave her such gifts—not the kind that were put in boxes, but the sort that filled her with imagination, breathing indescribable happiness into her life. One day, he built her a greenhouse. "So you can create your little monstrous plants," he explained.

He showed her how to catch the stray butterflies that fluttered from their elusive neighbors, who were rumored to farm them for cosmetic use. She would listen in morbid fascination as he described how the helpless insects were cruelly dismembered, before their fragile wings were crushed and ground into a fine powder. "Your lips would look beautiful, painted with butterfly wings," he would tease her.

"Never!" she'd cry, alarmed.

They spent much of their days alone, in their peaceful sanctuary, apart from the little visitor who came on weekends. When the weather was good, the three of them would venture out, past the worn jetty and picnic on their little beach. He would watch them proudly, marveling at the startling contrast between the two things he loved most in the world. His son with hair of spun gold, playing at his favorite rock pool and chattering animatedly in his singsong voice. She, with a small, amused smile on her tiny lips, raven hair tousled by the sea wind. She was different from anything he had ever known.

## The Keeper

You were like a dream,
    I wish I hadn't
    slept through.

Within it I fell deeper,
    than your heart would
    care to let you.

I thought you were a keeper,
    I wish I could
    have kept you.

## You

There are people I will never know
    and their lives will still ensue;
    those that could have loved me so
    and I'll never wonder who.

Of all the things to come and go,
    there is no one else like you.

The things I never think about—
    and the only thing I do.

## Us

I love him and he loves me.

We spend every moment together. When sleep parts us, we often meet in our dreams.

I like to take naps throughout the day. *Like a cat*, he says. He is a cat person.

He thinks my eyes are beautiful and strange. He has never seen eyes like mine up close before.

He says they look at him with daggers when he has done something wrong. Like when he forgets to order olives on my half of the pizza.

He thinks I am especially cute when angry.

We argue over whose turn it is to put the DVD in the player. Sometimes no one wins and we end up watching bad TV. Which is never really a bad thing.

He never imagined he would be with someone like me.

Now, he says, he can't imagine himself with anyone else.

. . . . . . . . . . . . . . . . . . . . . . . . . . . . . . .

We're kids, aren't we?
Yes, kids with grown-up powers.

## Swan Song

Her heart is played
    like well-worn strings;
    in her eyes,
    the sadness sings—
    of one who was destined
    for better things.

## DEAD POETS

Her poetry is written on the ghost of trees, whispered on the lips of lovers.

As a little girl, she would drift in and out of libraries filled with dead poets and their musky scent. She held them in her hands and breathed them in——wanting so much to be part of their world.

It wasn't long before Emily began speaking to her, then Sylvia and Katherine; their voices rang in unison, haunting and beautiful. They told her one day her poetry would be written on the ghost of trees and whispered on the lips of lovers.

But it would come at a price.

There isn't a thing I would not gladly give, she thought, to join my idols on those dusty shelves. To be immortal.

As if reading her mind, the voices of the dead poets cried out in alarm and warned her about the greatest heartache of all——how every stroke of pen thereafter would open the same wound over and over again.

What is the cause of such great heartache? She asked. They heard the keen anticipation in her voice and were sorry for her.

The greatest heartache comes from loving another soul, they said, beyond reason, beyond doubt, with no hope of salvation.

It was on her sixteenth birthday that she first fell in love. With a boy who brought her red roses and white lies. When he broke her heart, she cried for days.

Then hopeful, she sat with a pen in her hand, poised over the blank white sheet, but it refused to draw blood.

Many birthdays came and went.

One by one, she loved them and just as easily, they were lost to her. Somewhere amidst the carnations and forget-me-nots, between the lilacs and mistletoe—she slowly learned about love. Little by little, her heart bloomed into a bouquet of hope and ecstasy, of tenderness and betrayal.

Then she met you, and you brought her dandelions each day, so she would never want for wishes. She looked deep into your eyes and saw the very best of herself reflected back.

And she loved you, beyond reason, beyond doubt, and with no hope of salvation.

When she felt your love slipping away from her, she knelt at the altar, before all the great poets—and she begged. She no longer cared for poetry or immortality, she only wanted you.

But all the dead poets could do was look on, helpless and resigned while everything she had ever wished for came true in the cruelest possible way.

She learned too late that poets are among the damned, cursed to commiserate over their loss, to reach with outstretched hands— hands that will never know the weight of what they seek.

## LOST AND FOUND

A sunken chest,
  on the ocean ground,
  to never be found
  was where he found me.

There he stirred,
  my every thought,
  my every word,
  so gently, so profoundly.

Now I am kept,
  from dreams I dreamt,
  when once I slept,
  so soundly.

## Entwined

There is a line
    I'm yet to sever—
    it goes from me
    to you.

There was a time
    you swore forever,
    and I am captive
    to its pull.

If you were kind,
    you'd cut the tether—
    but I must ask you
    to be cruel.

## Soul Mates

I don't know how you are so familiar to me—or why it feels less like I am getting to know you and more as though I am remembering who you are. How every smile, every whisper brings me closer to the impossible conclusion that I have known you before, I have loved you before—in another time, a different place—some other existence.

## The Most

You may not know
    the reason why,
    for a time
    I wasn't I.

There was a man
    who came and went,
    on him every breath
    was spent.

I'm sorry I forgot
    all else—
    it was the most
    I ever felt.

## Sundays with Michael

I hold my breath and count to ten,
    I stand and sit, then stand again.
    I cross and then uncross my legs,
    the planes are flying overhead.

The dial turns with every twist,
    around the watch, around his wrist.
    Resting there with pen in hand,
    who could ever understand?

The way he writes of all I dream,
    things kind yet cruel and in-between,
    where underneath those twisted trees,
    a pretty girl fallen to her knees.

Who could know the world we've spun?
    I shrug my shoulders and hold my tongue.
    I hold my breath and count to ten,
    I stand and sit, then stand again.

## For You

Here are the things I want for you.

I want you to be happy. I want someone else to know the warmth of your smile, to feel the way I did when I was in your presence.

I want you to know how happy you once made me and though you really did hurt me, in the end, I was better for it. I don't know if what we had was love, but if it wasn't, I hope never to fall in love. Because of you, I know I am too fragile to bear it.

I want you to remember my lips beneath your fingers and how you told me things you never told another soul. I want you to know that I have kept sacred, everything you had entrusted in me and I always will.

Finally, I want you to know how sorry I am for pushing you away when I had only meant to bring you closer. And if I ever felt like home to you, it was because you were safe with me. I want you to know that most of all.

## Amends

I wonder if there will be a morning when you'll wake up missing me. That some incident in your life would have finally taught you the value of my worth. And you will feel a surge of longing, when you remember how I was good to you.

When this day comes I hope you will look for me. I hope you will look with the kind of conviction I'd always hoped for, but never had from you. Because I want to be found. And I hope it will be you—who finds me.

## A Way Out

Do you know what it is like,
    to lie in bed awake;
    with thoughts to haunt
    you every night,
    of all your past mistakes.

Knowing sleep will set it right—
    if you were not to wake.

## Dead Butterflies

I sometimes think about the fragility of glass—of broken shards tearing against soft skin. When in truth, it is the transparency that kills you. The pain of seeing through to something you can never quite touch.

For years I've kept you in secret, behind a glass screen. I've watched helplessly as day after day, your new girlfriend becomes your wife and then later, the mother of your children. Then realizing the irony in thinking you were the one under glass when in fact it has been me—a pinned butterfly—static and unmoving, watching while your other life unfolds.

## Lullabies

I barely know you, she says, voice heavy with sleep. I don't know your favorite color or how you like your coffee. What keeps you up at night or the lullabies that sing you to sleep. I don't know a thing about the first girl you loved, why you stopped loving her or why you still do.

I don't know how many millions of cells you are made of and if they have any idea they are part of something so beautiful and unimaginably perfect.

I may not have a clue about any of these things, but this——she places her hand on his chest——*this* I know.

## ALL THERE WAS

My greatest lesson learnt,
    you were mine until you weren't.

It was you who taught me so,
    the grace in letting go.

The time we had was all—
    there was not a moment more.

### Nostalgia

Do you remember our first day? The fog lifted and all around us were trees linking hands, like children playing.

Our first night, when you stood by the door, conflicted, as I sat there with my knees tucked under my chin, and smiling.

Then rainbows arching over and the most beautiful sunsets I have ever seen.

How the wind howls as the sea whispers, *I miss you*.

Come back to me.

## BEFORE THERE WAS YOU

When I used to look above,
    all I saw was sky;
    and every song
    that I would sing,
    I sung not knowing why.

All I thought and all I felt,
    was only just because,
    never was it ever you—
    until it was all there was.

## That Day

I remember our highs in hues,
    like the color of his eyes
    as the sun was setting;
    the pale of his hands in mine,
    and the blue of his smile.

I remember our sorrows in shades,
    like the gray of the shadows,
    which loomed that day,
    and the white in his lie
    when he promised to stay.

## Letting Him Go

There is a particular kind of suffering to be experienced when you love something greater than yourself. A tender sacrifice.

Like the pained silence felt in the lost song of a mermaid; or the bent and broken feet of a dancing ballerina. It is in every considered step I am taking in the opposite direction of you.

## Forget Me Not

The choice was once
    your choosing,
    before losing
    became my loss.
    I was there in
    your forgetting—
    until I was forgot.

## The Poet

*Why do you write?* he asked.

So I can take my love for you and give it to the world, I reply.

Because you won't take it from me.

## Always

You were you,
   and I was I;
   we were two
   before our time.

I was yours
   before I knew,
   and you have always
   been mine too.

## A Bad Day

When thoughts of all but one,
    are those I am keeping.

When sore though there is none,
    for whom I am weeping.

A curtain drawn before the sun,
    and I wish to go on sleeping.

### REASONS

I wish I knew why he left. What his reasons were. Why he changed his mind.

For all these years, I have turned it over in my head—all the possibilities—yet none of them make any sense.

And then I think, perhaps it was because he never loved me. But that makes the least sense of all.

## Thoughts

Dawn turns to day,
    as stars are dispersed;
    wherever I lay,
    I think of you first.

The sun has arisen,
    the sky, a sad blue.
    I quietly listen—
    the wind sings of you.

The thoughts we each keep,
    that are closest to heart,
    we think as we sleep—
    and you're always my last.

## Jealousy

It was the way
    you spoke about her.

With animosity, regret, disdain
    and underneath it all—
    just a hint of pride.

## Sad Songs

Once there was a boy who couldn't speak but owned a music box that held every song in all the world. One day he met a girl who had never heard a single melody in her entire life and so he played her his favorite song. He watched while her face lit up with wonder as the music filled the sky and the poetry of lyrics moved her in a way she had never felt before.

He would play his songs for her day after day and she would sit by him quietly—never seeming to mind that he could only speak to her through song. She loved everything he played for her, but of them all—she loved the sad songs best. So he began to play them more and more until eventually, sad songs were all she would hear.

One day, he noticed it had been a very long time since her last smile. When he asked her why, she took both his hands in hers and kissed them warmly. She thanked him for his gift of music and poetry but above all else—for showing her sadness because she had known neither of these things before him. But it was now time for her to go away—to find someone who could show her what happiness was.

. . . . . . . . . . . . . . . . . . . . . . . . . . . . . . . . .

Do you remember the song that was playing the night we met? No, but I remember every song I have heard since you left.

## ACCEPTANCE

There are things I miss
    that I shouldn't,
    and those I don't
    that I should.

Sometimes we want
    what we couldn't—
    sometimes we love
    who we could.

## Wallflower

Shrinking in a corner,
    pressed into the wall;
    do they know I'm present,
    am I here at all?

Is there a written rule book,
    that tells you how to be—
    all the right things to talk about—
    that everyone has but me?

Slowly I am withering—
    a flower deprived of sun;
    longing to belong to—
    somewhere or someone.

## A Timeline

You and I
    against a rule,
    set for us by time.

A marker drawn
    to show our end,
    etched into its line.

The briefest moment
    shared with you—
    the longest
    on my mind.

## ANGELS

It happens like this. One day you meet someone and for some inexplicable reason, you feel more connected to this stranger than anyone else—closer to them than your closest family. Perhaps because this person carries an angel within them—one sent to you for some higher purpose, to teach you an important lesson or to keep you safe during a perilous time. What you must do is trust in them—even if they come hand in hand with pain or suffering—the reason for their presence will become clear in due time.

Though here is a word of warning—you may grow to love this person but remember they are not yours to keep. Their purpose isn't to save you but to show you how to save yourself. And once this is fulfilled, the halo lifts and the angel leaves their body as the person exits your life. They will be a stranger to you once more.

. . . . . . . . . . . . . . . . . . . . . . . . . . . . . . . .

It's so dark right now, I can't see any light around me.
That's because the light is coming from you. You can't see it but everyone else can.

## He and I

When words run dry,
    he does not try,
    nor do I.

We are on par.

He just is,
    I just am,
    and we just are.

## Losing You

I used to think I couldn't go a day without your smile. Without telling you things and hearing your voice back.

Then, that day arrived and it was so damn hard but the next was harder. I knew with a sinking feeling it was going to get worse, and I wasn't going to be okay for a very long time.

Because losing someone isn't an occasion or an event. It doesn't just happen once. It happens over and over again. I lose you every time I pick up your favorite coffee mug; whenever that one song plays on the radio, or when I discover your old t-shirt at the bottom of my laundry pile.

I lose you every time I think of kissing you, holding you, or wanting you. I go to bed at night and lose you, when I wish I could tell you about my day. And in the morning, when I wake and reach for the empty space across the sheets, I begin to lose you all over again.

## The Things We Hide

And so,
    I have put away
    the photographs,
    every trace of you
    I know.

The things that seem
    to matter less,
    are the ones
    we put on show.

## Tsunamis

*Be careful about giving your heart too quickly,* I was told.
*Boys only have one thing on their minds,* they cautioned.

I don't know if he truly loves me—how can I be sure? I can't
say with any conviction that he won't break my heart—but how
could I have stopped him from taking what was already his?

He swept in like a tsunami, wave after wave, and I didn't stand a
chance. All those warnings, all the things they tried to prepare
me for—lost in an instant—to the enormity of what I felt.

## Always with Me

Your love I once surrendered,
    has never left my mind.

My heart is just as tender,
    as the day I called you mine.

I did not take you with me,
    but you were never left behind.

## More than Love

Love was cruel,
    as I stood proud;
    he showed me you
    and I was bowed.

He deftly dealt
    his swiftest blow—
    I fell further than,
    I was meant to go.

And he ashamed,
    of what he'd caused,
    knew from then,
    that I was yours.

That he, an echo
    and you, the sound—
    I loved you more
    than love allowed.

## First Love

Before I fell
in love with words,
with setting skies
and singing birds—
it was you I fell
in love with first.

## That Night

It was one of those nights that you are not altogether sure really did happen. There are no photographs, no receipts, no scrawled journal entries.

Just the memory sitting in my mind, like a half-blown dandelion, waiting to be fractured, dismembered. Waiting to disintegrate into nothing.

As I close my eyes, the pictures play like a blurry montage. I can see us driving for hours, until the street signs grew less familiar— the flickering lamplights giving away to stars. Then sitting across from you in that quiet, little Italian place. Your hands pushing the plates aside, reaching across for mine.

The conversations we had about everything and nothing. And kissing you. How I remember that.

It was one of those nights that my mind still can't be sure of. That wonders if I was ever there at all. Yet in my heart, it is as though I've never left.

## Déjà Vu

I saw it once,
    I have no doubt;
    but now can't place
    its whereabouts.

I try to think it,
    time and time;
    but what it is,
    won't come to mind.

A word, a scent—
    a feeling, past.
    It will not show,
    though much I've asked.

And when it comes,
    I soon forget—
    this is how it felt,
    when we first met.

## A Stranger

There is a love I reminisce,
    like a seed
    I've never sown.

Of lips that I am yet to kiss,
    and eyes
    not met my own.

Hands that wrap around my wrists,
    and arms
    that feel like home.

I wonder how it is I miss,
    these things
    I've never known.

## Signposts

What if certain people were signposts in your life? Representations of good or bad. Like an old friend you see across a crowded street, one you wave hello to, before hurrying on. The last time you saw them, things took a turn for the worse and, as sad as it may seem, they have unwittingly become an omen—a precursor of bad luck.

Or that one person whom you rarely speak with, who can always be found right where you left them. You carry their smile with you like a talisman—for whatever reason, their presence in your life will always bring the promise of better days.

Then there is the boy you can never stop thinking about. Whenever you see his name, it trips you up. Even if it's one that belongs to many others, even if he belongs to someone else.

You know he is a symbol of your weakness, your Kryptonite. How he rushes in like wildfire and burns through everything you worked so hard to build since he last left you in ashes.

So you do the only thing you know how—you put as many miles as you can between him. As many roadblocks and traffic lights as you can gather. Then you build a bold red stop sign right on your doorstep, knowing all the stop signs in the world could never hold him—they can only ask him to stay awhile.

## Clocks

Here in time,
    you are mine;
    my heart has not
    sung louder.

I do not know
    why I love you so—
    the clock knows not
    its hour.

Yet it is clear,
    to all that's here,
    that time is told
    by seeing.

Even though
    clocks do not know,
    it is the reason
    for their being.

## No Other

There is someone I keep in my heart—I love him and no one else. It is a love that will only die with me.

You may ask, *death could be some time away—what if from now to then, you love someone new?*

Well I can tell you, there is only one love. If any person claims to have loved twice in all their life—they have not loved at all.

## WISHFUL THINKING

You say that you are over me,
    my heart—
    it skips,
    it sinks.

I see you now with someone new,
    I stare,
    I stare,
    I blink.

Someday I'll be over you,
    I know,
    I know—
    I think.

## SOUNDTRACKS

He once told me about his love for lyrics. How the words spoke to him like poetry.

I would often wonder about his playlist and the ghosts who lived there. The faces he saw and the voices he heard. The soundtrack to a thousand tragic endings, real or imagined.

The first time I saw him, I noticed how haunted his eyes were. And I was drawn to him, in the way a melody draws a crowd to the dance floor. Pulled by invisible strings.

Now I wonder if I am one of those ghosts—if I am somewhere, drifting between those notes. I hope I am. I hope whenever my song plays, I am there, whispering in his ear.

## The End

"I don't know what to say," he said.

"It's okay," she replied, "I know what we are—and I know what we're not."

## Beach Ball

Do you know that feeling? When it's like you've lost something but can't remember what it was. It's as though you're trying so desperately to think of a word but it won't come to you. You've said it a thousand times before and it was always there—right where you left it. But now you can't recall it. You try and try to make it appear and it almost does, but it never does.

There are times when I think it could surface—when I sense it at the tip of my tongue. When I feel it struggling to burst from my chest like a beach ball that can only be held beneath the water for so long.

I can feel it stirring each time someone hurts me. When I smile at a stranger and they don't smile back. When I trust someone with a secret and they betray me. When someone I admire tells me I am not good enough.

I don't know what it is or what I have lost. But I know it was important, I know it once made me happy.

## Afraid to Love

I turn away
    and close my heart—
    to the promise of love
    that is luring.

For the past has taught
    to not be caught,
    in what is not
    worth pursuing—

To never do
    the things I've done
    that once had led
    to my undoing.

## Time

You were the one
    I wanted most
    to stay.

But time could not
    be kept at bay.

The more it goes,
    the more it's gone—
    the more it takes away.

## Wounded

A bruise is tender
  but does not last,
  it leaves me as
  I always was.

But a wound I take
  much more to heart,
  for a scar will always
  leave its mark.

And if you should ask
  which one you are,
  my answer is—
  you are a scar.

## Lost Things

Do you know when you've lost something—like your favorite t-shirt or a set of keys—and while looking for it, you come across something else you once missed but have long since forgotten? Well whatever it was, there was a point where you decided to stop searching, maybe because it was no longer required or a new replacement was found. It is almost as if it never existed in the first place—until that moment of rediscovery, a flash of recognition.

Everyone has one—an inventory of lost things waiting to be found. Yearning to be acknowledged for the worth they once held in your life.

I think this is where I belong—among all your other lost things. A crumpled note at the bottom of a drawer or an old photograph pressed between the pages of a book. I hope someday you will find me and remember what I once meant to you.

## THE GIRL HE LOVES

There was a man who I once knew,
    for me there was no other.
    The closer to loving me he grew,
    the more he would grow further.

I tried to love him as his friend,
    then to love him as his lover;
    but he never loved me in the end—
    his heart was for another.

## Patience

Patience and Love agreed to meet at a set time and place; beneath the twenty-third tree in the olive orchard. Patience arrived promptly and waited. She checked her watch every so often but still, there was no sign of Love.

Was it the twenty-third tree or the fifty-sixth? She wondered and decided to check, just in case. As she made her way over to the fifty-sixth tree, Love arrived at twenty-three, where Patience was noticeably absent.

Love waited and waited before deciding he must have the wrong tree and perhaps it was another where they were supposed to meet.

Meanwhile, Patience had arrived at the fifty-sixth tree, where Love was still nowhere to be seen.

Both begin to drift aimlessly around the olive orchard, almost meeting but never do.

Finally, Patience, who was feeling lost and resigned, found herself beneath the same tree where she began. She stood there for barely a minute when there was a tap on her shoulder.

It was Love.

. . . . . . . . . . . . . . . . . . . . . . . . . . . . . . . .

"Where are you?" she asked. "I have been searching all my life."
"Stop looking for me," Love replied, "and I will find you."

## Second Chances

The path from you extending,
　　I could not see its course—
　　or the closer to you I was getting,
　　the further from you I'd walked.

For I was moving in a circle,
　　not a line as I had thought—
　　the steps I took away from you,
　　were taking me towards.

## Dyslexia

There were letters I wrote you that I gave up sending, long before I stopped writing. I don't remember their contents, but I can recall with absolute clarity, your name scrawled across the pages. I could never quite contain you to those messy sheets of blue ink. I could not stop you from overtaking everything else.

I wrote your name over and over—on scraps of paper, in books and on the back of my wrists. I carved it like sacred markings into trees and the tops of my thighs. Years went by and the scars have vanished, but the sting has not left me. Sometimes when I read a book, parts will lift from the pages in an anagram of your name. Like a code to remind me it's not over. Like dyslexia in reverse.

## ALL OR NOTHING

If you love me
  for what you see,
  only your eyes would be
  in love with me.

If you love me
  for what you've heard,
  then you would love me
  for my words.

If you love
  my heart and mind,
  then you would love me,
  for all that I'm.

But if you don't love
  my every flaw,
  then you mustn't love me—
  not at all.

## Metamorphosis

I am somebody else's story. The girl who served their drink, the person they pushed past on a crowded street, the one who broke their heart. I have happened in so many places, to so many people—the essence of me lives on in these nuances, these moments.

Yet never have I been bolder or brighter than I am with you. Not once have I ever felt so alive. Whatever vessel we pour ourselves into, mine is now overflowing, brimming with life. It is transcending into something new.

Hands are no longer hands. They are caresses. Mouths are no longer mouths. They are kisses. My name is no longer a name, it is a call. And love is no longer love—love is you.

## HER WORDS

Love a girl who writes
    and live her many lives;
    you have yet to find her,
    beneath her words of guise.

Kiss her blue-inked fingers,
    forgive the pens they marked.
    The stain of your lips upon her—
    the one she can't discard.

Forget her tattered memories,
    or the pages others took;
    you are her ever after—
    the hero of her book.

## Closure

Like time suspended,
    a wound unmended—
    you and I.

We had no ending,
    no said good-bye.

For all my life,
    I'll wonder why.

## Acknowledgments

Thank you to Al Zuckerman and Writers House for your ongoing guidance and support.

To Kirsty and her team at Andrews McMeel for your passion and dedication.

To Ollie Faudet, the little oracle.

To my family and friends with all my love.

To my readers, words cannot express how much your support means to me.

## About the Author

The work of poet and artist Lang Leav swings between the whimsical and woeful, expressing a complexity beneath its childlike facade.

Lang is a recipient of the Qantas Spirit of Youth Award and a prestigious Churchill Fellowship.

Her artwork is exhibited internationally and she was selected to take part in the landmark Playboy Redux show curated by the Andy Warhol Museum.

She currently lives with her partner and collaborator, Michael, in a little house by the sea.

# INDEX

POSTED POEMS

Posted Poems is a unique postal service that allows you to send your favorite Lang Leav poem to anyone, anywhere in the world. All poems are printed on heavyweight art paper and encased in a beautiful string-tie envelope. To send a Posted Poem to someone special visit: langleav.com/postedpoems

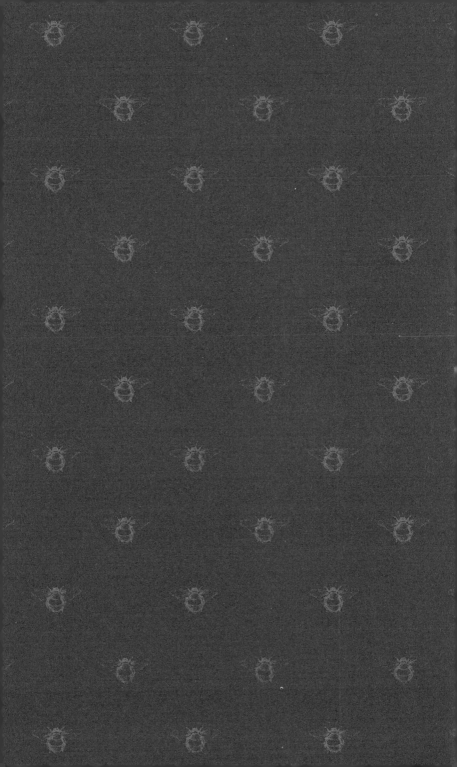